Obadiah's Christmas

By Tink Leonard
Illustrations by Audrey Cortez

atlanta book printing

©2012 by Tink Leonard

Printed in the USA
ISBN: 978-0-9829006-9-7

To my
daughter, Kelli.

This is for you.

Obadiah's Christmas

And it came to pass in those days, that there went out a decree from Caesar Augustus, that all the world should be taxed. (And this taxing was first made when Cyrenius was governor of Syria). And all went to be taxed, every one into his own city. And Joseph also went up from Galilee, out of the city of Nazareth, into Judea, unto the city of David, which is called Bethlehem (because he was of the house and lineage of David), to be taxed with Mary, his espoused wife, being great with child. And so it was, that, while they were there, the days were accomplished that she should be delivered. And she brought forth her first-born son, and wrapped him in swaddling clothes, and laid him in a manger; because there was no room for them in the inn. *Luke 2:1-7, KJV*

"Oh, hello, my name is Obadiah, which means servant of the Lord. You probably never heard of me, but I was in the stable when Jesus was born. I'm the stable cat."

"What?" you say. "There was no cat in the stable!"

"Of course there was. Just think about it. There were cattle, so there was hay, which meant, of course, there were mice, so there had to be a cat, and I am he. We were all there: the little lamb, the mice, the cattle, the donkey, and, of course, me. Anyway, now that we have cleared that up, let us tell you the story."

"The shepherds had come into the stable with a
newborn lamb and one of the old sheep dogs. It was
too dark and cold a night to leave the little lamb out
in the field. The shepherd laid the lamb beside the
old dog on the hay to stay warm, and the little lamb
told me the story of the angels."

The shepherds were in the field watching over us, as there were always wolves in the area. I was a little afraid, but my mother told me the shepherds would keep us safe. I was almost asleep when suddenly there was a bright light that seemed to be everywhere. It was shining so brightly, and there was a song coming from it. The night wind carried the song through the trees to where I lay in the field.

The shepherds were afraid because of the great light and the sound. Out of the light came an angel. I didn't know it was an angel at the time, because I didn't know what an angel was, so I asked the old sheep dog. I knew he would know because he was so much older and wiser. He was at least six years old.

I asked him, "What is that?"

"That is an angel, little one," the dog said.

"What is angel?" I asked him.

"An angel is a messenger of the Lord," he said.
"Something very important is going to happen."

audrey Cortez

The angel said to the shepherds,

"Do not be afraid, for I bring you good news of great joy that will be for all the people. For unto you is born this day in the city of David, a savior, which is Christ the Lord. And this shall be a sign unto you: ye shall find the babe wrapped in swaddling clothes and lying in a manger."

And suddenly there was with the angel a host of angels, praising God and saying:

"Glory to God in the highest, and on earth peace, good will toward men." *Luke 2:10-14, NIV*

Then just as suddenly, the angels were gone.

When the angels left, one of the shepherds picked me up and said to the others,

"Let us go to Bethlehem and see this thing that has happened."

So the shepherds came to the stable and saw the baby as the angel had told them.

That is the story the little lamb told me, but there was more that happened that night.

I was back in the hay so no one would see me, but I could see the baby. He looked like every baby, I suppose, though I will say I had never seen a baby in the stable. But there was something special about him. There seemed to be a great peace around him. I looked up and saw the angel the lamb told me about, shining brightly over the baby as if guarding him. I could hear the angels singing as the little lamb had heard out in the field. When I looked at the little lamb, he was watching very carefully, and it looked like he was singing with the angels. I couldn't really tell because I never heard a lamb sing.

There were also mice in the stable with me. (We've already talked about the mice and the hay, remember?)

A little mouse called Thaddeus asked the angel, "Who is this baby that angels would guard him, and the song of heaven would be heard on earth?"

The angel then told us the story of the angel Gabriel and Mary, the mother of Jesus:

God sent the angel Gabriel to Nazareth, a town in Galilee, to a virgin named Mary, who was pledged to be married to a man named Joseph. The angel came to her and said, "Hail, you who are highly favored, the Lord is with you, blessed are you among women."

"Now Mary was afraid that an angel would speak to her and did not understand his greeting or what it might mean. But the angel said to her,

"Do not be afraid, Mary, you have found favor with God. You will be with child and give birth to a son, and you are to give him the name Jesus. He will be great and will be called the Son of the Most High. The Lord God will give him the throne of his father David, and he will reign over the house of Jacob forever, and his kingdom will never end." Luke 2:26-33, NIV

"I am the Lord's servant," Mary answered. "May it be to me as you have said." Luke 2:38, NIV

All this took place to fulfill what the Lord had said through the prophets: 'The virgin will be with child and will give birth to a son, and they will call him Immanuel' – which means "God with us." Matt. 1:23, NIV

And then, as with the shepherds, the angel left her.

"I will never forget that night," said the little mouse. *"The angel told us that the Messiah had come at last. But, as I looked to see the Messiah, all I could see was a sleeping baby."*

I thought about what Thaddeus had said, but all I could think was,

"Surely that's not right; whoever heard of a baby Messiah?"

Thaddeus continued, "I heard people talk of the Messiah, and this was not the Messiah, at least not the one they were expecting. They talked of the Messiah, the King of the Jews they called him, as being strong and who would return their nation to greatness and deliver them from their enemies."

"There was something in the air that said this is the Messiah, this is Emmanuel, the one we have waited for so long. He will deliver his people and his kingdom will never end."

"I believed this," said Thaddeus, "although I did not know how a baby could save anyone, but the angel said he was the Messiah, so I believed."

Audrey Cortez

"I believed too," said the donkey. "I carried the mother across the desert for over 70 miles. It took a long time. I could tell she was very tired and when we got into town, I was glad because I was tired too."

"There were so many people in town and there was no room for them at the inn. There was only the stable. That was fine with me, but people didn't usually sleep in the stable, and she was going to have a baby."

"What about me?" another voice said. "Even though I wasn't at the stable, I do know about the baby Messiah."

"Who said that?" asked Thaddeus.

"I did."

We turned around to see who was talking and then kept looking up. It was something really big.

I asked very softly, "Who, or what, are you?"

"My name is Deborah, and I'm a camel."

"What do you know about the baby Messiah if you weren't at the stable when the angel came, and when the shepherds came?" asked the donkey.

"I saw the star," said Deborah.

'What star?" asked the lamb. "We only saw the angels and heard the song of heaven."

"Well," said Deborah, "I didn't see any angels, and I didn't hear any singing, but I did see the star. It was in the eastern sky and was very beautiful and very bright. The Magi had been following the star when we came to Jerusalem."

"I've been to Jerusalem," said the donkey. "I didn't like it."

Deborah continued, "We went to Jerusalem to find out about the Messiah, the King of the Jews. The Magi knew something important was happening, so we stopped in Jerusalem to get directions, more or less. I heard the Magi say the king there was very helpful and had asked that when they found this new King of the Jews, to come and tell him so he could also go and worship him."

"We followed the star until it stopped over the place where the child was. On entering the house, they saw the child with his mother, and they bowed down and worshipped him. They presented him with gifts of gold, frankincense and myrrh. We didn't go back through Jerusalem because the Magi were warned in a dream not to go that way."

This is the story of the birth of Jesus as told by the ones who were there.

And Jesus said, "These words are trustworthy and true. And the Lord, the God of the spirits of the prophets, has sent his angel to show his servants what must soon take place. "

"And behold, I am coming soon."

Rev. 22: 6-7 (RSV)